We Could Be Famous

Story by George Ivanoff
Illustrations by Whitney Lam

We Could Be Famous

Text: George Ivanoff
Publishers: Tania Mazzeo and Eliza Webb
Series consultant: Amanda Sutera
Hands on Heads Consulting
Editor: Jess Mackay
Project editor: Annabel Smith
Designer: Jess Kelly
Project designer: Danielle Maccarone
Illustrations: Whitney Lam
Production controller: Renee Tome

NovaStar

ISBN 978 0 17 033489 1

Cengage Learning Australia
Level 5, 80 Dorcas Street
Southbank VIC 3006 Australia
Phone: 1300 790 853
Email: aust.nelsonprimary@cengage.com

For learning solutions, visit **cengage.com.au**

Printed in China by 1010 Printing International Ltd
1 2 3 4 5 6 7 29 28 27 26 25

Nelson acknowledges the Traditional Owners and Custodians of the lands of all First Nations Peoples. We pay respect to Elders past and present, and extend that respect to all First Nations Peoples today.

Contents

Chapter 1

4–Eva Cool

The crowd broke into a frenzied roar as the song ended. The four performers each dropped to one knee at the edge of the stage, as the final note sounded. It was flawlessly choreographed.

"This clip was uploaded last night," said Bobby. He grinned, his eyes sparkling with excitement. "I've already watched it way too many times."

"Aren't they wonderful," Lily said with a sigh.

"They've got great voices," agreed Bobby. "They sound perfect together, especially on the harmonies."

Zac nodded his agreement, his floppy fringe of blond hair falling over his eyes. He flicked it back.

"And their moves," added August, "are perfectly in sync."

Bobby and his three friends were huddled around a tablet watching the latest concert clip from their favourite band, 4-Eva Cool. They were on a break from their Saturday morning singing class, doing what they always did during their breaks – watching music videos and concert clips.

"I wish we sounded that good," said Bobby, wistfully.

"We will," said August. "One day."

"Our singing is already so much better since starting these classes," agreed Lily.

"But we're still nothing like 4-Eva Cool," said Bobby. "I don't see any screaming fans waiting for us outside."

"That's cos we don't have any music videos," said August, sagely. "Or sold-out concerts."

Lily laughed. "We don't even have a song."

Just then, Zac got a faraway look in his eyes. "Maybe we should," he whispered.

"Should what?" asked Lily.

"Maybe we should have a song?"

Bobby, Lily and August all turned to stare at their friend. "What?" they said in unison.

"We should record a song together," insisted Zac.

Lily laughed. "Yeah ... right."

"We're not good enough," said Bobby, shaking his head.

Zac shrugged. "I reckon it'd be fun."

August and Lily looked at each other.

"We're ready," Mr Lennon called from the classroom where the other kids had all gathered to resume the lesson.

Any further discussion of recording a song stopped as the four friends rushed back to their singing class.

Bobby, Lily and August all went back to Zac's place after singing class. Zac's house had a large rumpus room in the basement, with a pinball machine, air-hockey table and a massive television. It was a good space to hang out; there was always something to do. Zac's dad had made them sandwiches for lunch.

"I'm serious," insisted Zac. "We should record a song together. It would be so cool."

Bobby laughed nervously, as if what Zac had just said was a joke, but inside he felt a little thrill of excitement. It *would* be cool to record a song ... but he couldn't say that out loud. He had the weakest voice out of the four of them. Surely they wouldn't really want him recording a song with them. He ran a hand through his dark curls and looked away.

"If we did record a song," said August, tentatively, "we could ... maybe ... put it online."

"AudioStreams!" Lily exclaimed. "It's a music streaming site where people can listen to music for free. There's heaps of cool stuff on the site. And people can leave comments and likes. I could set up an account easily enough and upload what we record." She nudged Bobby. "Then we'll have screaming fans waiting for us when we come out of singing class."

The suggestion hung in the air between the friends as they all fell silent. They chewed on their sandwiches, deep in thought. Bobby watched their faces, wondering what each of them was thinking. Were they actually serious?

"You know," said August, pushing their glasses further up the bridge of their nose. "4-Eva Cool got their start on AudioStreams."

Everyone stopped chewing and stared at them.

August took their glasses off and cleaned the lenses on their shirt. "4-Eva Cool recorded the band's first song in their parents' garage and put it up on AudioStreams. They got like a zillion likes and went viral."

August continued talking while wiping their glasses. “And the next thing you know, 4-Eva Cool had record companies offering them contracts. And then the band was off touring the world, performing concerts and being famous.”

August put their glasses back on to be met by the amazed looks of their friends.

"Well ... it's true," said August, with a shrug.

"We could be famous," whispered Lily.

Bobby looked from one friend to the next. They all wanted to do it. He could see the enthusiasm on their faces. And suddenly, he could feel the excitement bubbling up inside of him as well, pushing aside his doubts and insecurities.

"Let's do it!" he shouted.

Suddenly, all four friends were whooping and hollering, jumping around the room chanting, "Let's make a song! Let's make a song! Let's make a song!"

Chapter 2

Shakespeare?

"What are we going to sing?" asked Bobby, full of nervous excitement.

It was Sunday, and the four friends were gathered again in Zac's rumpus room.

"We could just pick our favourite 4-Eva Cool song," suggested Lily.

"Nah," said Bobby. "Covers of other people's songs never get as much attention as original songs do."

"We don't have any original songs," Lily reminded him.

"We could write one," said August. "We could write an awesome song together."

"I could write the music," said Bobby, "but I'm not sure I could come up with any lyrics."

"Don't look at me," said Lily. "I'm hopeless at writing."

Zac shrugged with his head down over his sketchbook, fringe almost brushing the paper. Everyone knew that drawing, not writing, was his thing.

"I like writing poems," said August. "I guess I could give lyrics a go. It's kinda the same thing."

"Cool!" Lily nodded her approval. "So what should the song be about?"

A barrage of suggestions followed – from school and friendship to video games and sports.

Everyone fell silent to consider the possibilities. Then August spoke up …

“Shakespeare!”

“What?” Bobby looked at August in wonder.

“We should write a song about William Shakespeare,” said August.

“Why?” asked Lily.

“Because we need something unexpected,” said August. “We need something a bit different.” They paused and looked down. “And it’d be cool.”

“There is nothing cool about Shakespeare,” said Lily.

“No one’s going to want to hear a song full of ‘thees’ and ‘thous’ and ‘thys’,” said Bobby in a posh accent.

August paused to take a deep breath before launching into an explanation. They told the group that Shakespeare had invented a lot of words and phrases that had become part of the English language. Terms like "wild goose chase" and "cold-blooded". Phrases like "melted into thin air" and "all that glitters is not gold". Even simple words like "uncomfortable". Shakespeare had taken the word "comfortable" and added an "un" to the start of it, creating a new word. It was in a play called *Romeo and Juliet*.

"Wow!" Zac looked impressed.

"No wonder you're top of the class in English," said Lily.

"Okay," concluded Bobby. "Let's give it a go."

Chapter 3

All That Glitters

The following Saturday, the moment singing class finished, Bobby, Zac, Lily and August raced over to Zac's house and barricaded themselves inside the rumpus room. Bobby whipped out his tablet and showed the others what he and August had been working on.

By midway through the week, August had sent a draft of the lyrics to Bobby. Bobby was really impressed; August was a talented lyricist. Bobby had then used a music app to compose a basic melody for the song and then recorded himself singing the lyrics. Finally, Bobby and August came up with the song title together. They called it "All That Glitters".

Bobby played the track for the others. His voice faltered over some of the higher notes and his timing was a little out, but it wasn't bad for a first demo.

"It'll sound better when Zac is singing the main part. And then Lily and August can do the harmonies and I'll do the backing vocals." Bobby paused and then powered on. "We can also do more work on the music. It's still a bit basic."

August quickly jumped in. "And I've got a few changes to the lyrics. If any of you want to make other changes to the words, that's fine, too."

"Wow!" said Zac.

"Yeah," agreed Lily. "Wow!"

"You like it?" asked Bobby, tentatively.

"Like it?" said Zac. "I love it!"

"Me too," agreed Lily.

"So what do we do now?" asked August. They looked expectantly at Bobby.

Bobby looked at the smiling faces of his friends, their enthusiasm encouraging him. "We make it even better."

The four friends spent the whole afternoon working on the song. They tweaked the melody and changed some of the words to work better with the music. Lily ran home to get her guitar and harmonica so they could add some real instrument sounds to the music that Bobby had created with the music app.

Bobby had borrowed a good microphone from Mr Lennon. The rumpus room in the basement was quiet, cut off from all the noise above. It was the perfect place for a makeshift recording studio.

After he set up the microphone, Bobby recorded separate tracks of Lily playing her guitar and harmonica, and then each of them singing their parts. Zac even fetched some pots and pans from the kitchen to add a bit of live percussion.

It was all coming together!

That evening, Bobby played the final version of "All That Glitters" to his parents.

"That's really good," said Bobby's mum. "I'm seriously impressed."

Bobby wondered if he detected surprise in her voice.

"Yes," agreed Bobby's dad. "It sounds really professional. Like it's been recorded with fancy equipment."

"I borrowed a good mic from singing class," explained Bobby.

Then he took a deep breath and made the big announcement. "We're going to release it on AudioStreams."

"Really?" There was a hint of something in Dad's voice that made Bobby pause.

"Isn't that a social media site?" asked Mum.

"Well, yeah," said Bobby. "But it's used specially for music. Lots of bands and singers get their start by putting music on AudioStreams for free."

"I don't think that's a good idea," said Mum. "We've talked about this before. You're not old enough to be on social media yet. And I certainly don't want you putting your personal details, including your name, on a public site."

"I agree," said Dad. "There's a lot of bullying and stalking on social media."

"But we've worked so hard on the song," pleaded Bobby. "We've got to put it online."

Mum shook her head and looked at Dad. "Definitely not," he agreed.

I have to find a way to convince them, thought Bobby.

And then he had a brilliant idea.

Chapter 4

4–Eva Unknown

"My parents told me 'no' as well," said Lily.

"Same here," said August.

Zac just nodded sadly.

It was the next morning, on Sunday, and the friends were gathered in Zac's rumpus room discussing what their parents had said the night before.

"But then," continued Bobby, "I came up with an idea." He grinned. "And so they said yes!"

"What?" asked Lily.

Bobby explained that they could upload their song without any of their personal details – not even their names. They would be anonymous.

"But we can't," said August. "AudioStreams won't let you put any music online unless you have a profile."

"Actually, there is a way," said Lily.

She pulled her tablet out of her bag, brought up the AudioStreams app and showed them.

It was possible – all they had to do was create a band profile. With a band profile, you didn't have to enter all the same details as on a personal profile. Lily's fingers flew across the screen, tapping away, setting up their new profile.

August pointed to the screen. "But we still need to enter our names."

"They can be aliases," said Bobby. "Stage names. Like Lady Gaga or Lizzo." He leaned over Lily's shoulder and entered "Bee-Bee" instead of Bobby Benton.

Lily grinned and entered "Flower Girl" for herself, then looked at August.

August looked thoughtful for a moment, then said, "How about 'July'?"

They all laughed, and Lily added the name. Then they all looked up at Zac. He reached for the tablet and entered "muZak".

"What about profile pics?" asked Lily, taking the tablet back. "My mum would freak out if I put my photo online."

"I can do cartoon drawings," suggested Zac, as he grabbed his sketchbook that was nearby.

His pencil flew across the page, then he held up a quick sketch of a microphone with a face and floppy hair. “Say hi to muZak.”

They all laughed.

“So then, what we need is a band name,” said Lily. “How about Anony-mouse?”

“Too obvious,” Bobby replied.

“Since we were inspired by 4-Eva Cool,” said August, “what about ‘4-Eva Awesome’?”

"Or '4-Eva Unknown'," mumbled Zac, as he continued sketching.

"I like that," said Lily.

"Me too," agreed August.

"Cool," said Bobby. "4-Eva Unknown. That's us!" He grinned at his friends. "So ... are we ready to do this?"

"Definitely!" replied the others in unison.

Lily uploaded "All That Glitters". 4-Eva Unknown's first song was officially released!

When Bobby walked through the school gate on Monday morning, Lily barrelled up to him. She grabbed him by the shoulders and stared into his face.

"Have you checked 'All That Glitters' on AudioStreams?" she asked.

"Relax," said Bobby. "I looked at it before bed last night. We had about ninety streams. Which is not bad since it only went up yesterday."

"But have you checked it *this morning*?" Lily had a goofy grin on her face.

"No," admitted Bobby. "I slept in and had to hurry to get to school on time."

Lily dug out her tablet from her school bag and held it up for Bobby to see.

Bobby's eyes widened. "No way!"

"Hey," called August as they walked through the gate. "What's up?"

"It's been streamed over TEN THOUSAND TIMES!" Bobby's voice was breathless. "And it hasn't even been 24 hours!"

August grabbed the tablet and stared at it. "O … M … G!"

Zac approached, holding his own tablet high above his head, a huge smile on his face. "I think we're almost famous!"

The bell rang to signal the start of first class and, with barely contained excitement, the friends agreed to meet up at Zac's place after school.

"We're up to 570 117 streams!" said Bobby with astonishment.

The four friends tore around the rumpus room, hollering and cheering and laughing.

"So does this mean we've gone viral?" asked August, once they had settled down again.

"I think you need more than a million streams to go viral," said Lily thoughtfully. "The big question is: do the people listening to our song actually like it?"

Bobby checked the AudioStreams stats. "We've got 304 099 likes and just over 1000 dislikes. So more people like it than hate it."

"What about the comments?" asked August.

"Never read the comments," suggested Zac. "You should have them turned off."

Bobby ignored Zac's advice and started going through the comments. "Lots of really great ones. Stuff like '*Fab song!*', '*Awesome!*' and '*You guys are the BEST!*'"

"Anything negative?" asked Zac.

"Well ..." Bobby hesitated. "There are a few. But nothing too bad."

"Like what?" asked August, a nervous look on their face.

"Check out this comment," burst out Bobby, ignoring his friend's question. "*Great song! All that glitters may not be gold, but this song certainly is! Best thing on AudioStreams. When's the next one?*" Bobby looked up at the others.

"We don't have a next one," said Lily.

"Yet!" corrected Bobby.

"Actually ..." All eyes turned to look at August. "I may have started writing another one already."

Chapter 5

The Follow-Up Song

Two weeks later, Bobby finally hit the upload button. "Aaaaand … it's up!"

"Thank goodness," said Lily. "I didn't think we'd ever get this one done."

Bobby sighed. It had taken the friends a long time to finish the new song. "All That Glitters" had come together so easily and was so much fun to make. But with this one, the group had argued about everything – the topic, the lyrics, the music, what instruments to use, who would sing which bit. The group had even thrown out August's first attempt, which was about Shakespeare's play *A Midsummer Night's Dream*. They couldn't agree on whether it was cool enough or not. In the end, they all collaborated on writing the lyrics for a song about school being boring.

The friends felt the pressure building. Their first song continued to be *really* popular on AudioStreams. By the time they finished their second song, the first one had reached over 5 million streams. But the number of dislikes it was getting increased, too. The ratio between likes and dislikes was now about half-half. And there were lots more negative comments:

Still no follow-up song. This is a one-hit wonder group.

Only one song. And it's not gold. What a bunch of losers.

Just listened to this song. Ha! No wonder they want to keep their identities a secret.

If I'd made this, I wouldn't tell anyone who I was either.

All these comments were disheartening. The friends found it harder and harder to get enthusiastic about the new song. But they also felt like they had to make a second song ... if only to prove their critics wrong.

The group had struggled through their disagreements to finally finish "Classroom Boredom". They uploaded it on Sunday afternoon before the new school week.

"Now what?" asked Bobby. "Do we celebrate? Or should we start working on a third song?"

Zac shook his head.

"Do we have to do another?" whined Lily. She sounded as if it were the last thing in the world that she wanted to do.

"We're sort of famous now," said Bobby. "We probably should do another one."

"Not today," said Lily.

"I'm exhausted," announced August. "And I need to get home."

When Bobby walked through the school gate on Monday morning, Lily was waiting for him again. She barrelled up to him, but this time she had a different look on her face.

"No, I haven't looked," Bobby said, before she'd had the chance to ask. "I slept in – again."

Lily opened her mouth to speak, but August came racing up to them. They were wild-eyed and looked slightly panicked. "Oh gosh, oh gosh, oh gosh. Have you seen?"

"No, I haven't," said Bobby with a smirk. "Have we gone viral again?"

"Not really," said Lily.

"So … what then?" Bobby looked confused.

"We've got a couple of thousand streams," explained August. "But it's the comments."

"What's up?" asked Zac, as he strolled up to the others.

"You might want to take a look," said Lily, holding up her tablet.

Zac glanced over Lily's shoulder. "Oh."

Bobby took hold of the device and stared at the first comment on the screen:

They're not 4-Eva Unknown …
they're 4-Eva Garbage!

By lunchtime, the new song had over 2000 dislikes, but only a couple of hundred likes. And the negative comments continued. They got worse and worse. It seemed like most people hated their new song. But the comments weren't just about the song. People were saying awful things about their voices, about their stage names, about their cartoon profile pics and about personal things they couldn't possibly know about.

People were also going back to their first song, rating it with a dislike and adding negative comments about it as well.

Bobby switched off the comments on both their songs and on the band profile, so that new ones couldn't be added. By the time the end-of-lunch bell rang, he was almost in tears.

"That's it!" said Lily. "I don't want to do any more songs."

The four friends were all gathered in the school library to talk about what they were going to do.

"I don't ever want to write a song again," whispered August, their eyes downcast.

"I don't want to sing any more," added Bobby.

"What?" Zac looked at him with concern. "You can't stop singing just because some people don't like our song."

"My voice got the worst comments," Bobby almost shouted. "They all hate me!"

"Dude ..." Zac shook his head slowly. "*Never* read the comments."

"I know you've turned off the comments," said August, "but can we delete the ones that are already there?"

"I don't know," said Bobby. "I'll have to check."

"Um ... guys," interrupted Lily. "You might want to take a look at this. We're on the 'What's What in Pop' blog."

"Can you read it out?" asked Bobby without enthusiasm.

Lily read the blog post to her friends.

Is Mystery Band a Joke?

A couple of weeks ago, a mystery band took AudioStreams by storm. But the release of their second song now has listeners wondering if they really exist.

Calling themselves "4-Eva Unknown", four mystery individuals released their first song on the AudioStreams free music platform. "All That Glitters" went viral with over a million streams in just a few days. Clever lyrics combined with a catchy tune resulted in an overwhelmingly positive response. While the song certainly wasn't pop brilliance, it was definitely likeable.

But their second song, "Classroom Boredom", saw a complete turnaround with listeners savaging it in the comments. It has none of the charm, wit or intelligence of the first song and is musically bland. It feels like it's been written by a bunch of kids.

If this is the quality of their songwriting, is that first one even theirs? That's what listeners are asking. Who are these mystery musicians? Did they really write and record these songs? Or is it all a massive joke, created with AI and placed on AudioStreams to fool the listeners?

“This is getting worse,” mumbled August.

“What are we going to do?” asked Lily.

Bobby stood up and looked at his friends. “I reckon we ask our parents for help.”

Chapter 6

Help

"Maybe I should delete the account," said Bobby. "Just get rid of everything."

Bobby was sitting in the lounge room with his parents that evening. He had just told them everything that had happened and read out some of the negative comments.

"You could do that," said Dad. "But your songs have already been listened to by millions of people around the world. And some of those people might have copied the songs. Even if you delete the account, these people will still have your music. Once something is on the internet, it's out in the world forever. You can't get rid of it completely. If you close your account, what's to stop someone else from putting your songs back online?"

"Oh." Bobby felt miserable.

"Think of this as a learning experience," said Mum, thoughtfully. "No one knows who you are. Yes, there were lots of nasty comments, but remember ... these people don't know you. They have no idea what you're really like. Their opinions aren't worth anything."

"And also remember," added Dad, "that lots of people loved your songs. Just think about all those people who are listening to and still liking something that you and your friends created. That's something to be proud of."

"Okay," said Bobby. "We're all agreed. We'll delete the comments but leave the songs up."

Lily, August and Zac nodded. The four friends, having spoken to their parents the night before, were now gathered in the library before the start of school.

"And we'll never do anything like this ever again," declared Lily.

"But …" August looked at Lily. "I really liked singing with all of you. And writing lyrics was fun."

"We don't have to stop doing that," said Bobby. "We just don't need to put our stuff online."

"Actually …" said Zac, "I reckon we put up one more song."

"What?" Everyone said in unison, gaping at Zac.

"Hear me out," he insisted. "I had a long talk with my parents about all this. About how the first song was fun, but the second one wasn't. About all the pressure once the song was online. And about the comments. They were horrible and unfair and … well … people were bullying us, just cos they could. So …"

He paused and took a long, deep breath. "Let's write a song about what happened to us. About the comments. About how it stopped being fun. About how unfair people were."

Chapter 7

The Final Song

A week later, 4-Eva Unknown uploaded their final song onto AudioStreams, along with the following message:

A few weeks ago, we shared our very first song, "All That Glitters", on AudioStreams. We had lots of fun creating it and we were very excited to share it with the world. People seemed to like it. But then we started to get all sorts of nasty comments from people who don't even know us.

Some of you wondered why we stayed anonymous. It's because we're just a group of school friends and our parents didn't want us putting our details online. And they were right. We started doing this because we thought it would be fun. We got the idea from our favourite band, 4-Eva Cool. They got their start on AudioStreams, so we thought we might give it a go.

But it's not fun any more. So this is our last song. We hope you enjoy "Thoughtless Comments".

Two days later, Dad announced, "You made the news."

"Huh?" Bobby looked up bleary-eyed over the breakfast table.

Dad had a huge grin on his face as he propped his mobile phone up in front of Bobby. *Thoughtful Song Makes the Music World Take Notice* was the lead video in the entertainment section of the news site. Dad clicked on it and the reporter started talking.

“A talented group of kids calling themselves 4-Eva Unknown have turned a negative situation into something positive, using their third and final song, ‘Thoughtless Comments’, to draw attention to online bullying,” the reporter said.

“ ‘Thoughtless Comments’ has gone viral, with even more people streaming it than their previous songs combined. The band has switched off comments on their profile, but it hasn’t stopped their fans from making their feelings known.

“Thousands of emails have been sent to AudioStreams praising the new song and begging 4-Eva Unknown to release more music. The song has even prompted the pop group 4-Eva Cool to release a press statement in which the band members revealed that they too struggled with thoughtless comments, particularly when they first began recording music.

“It seems like 4-Eva Unknown, whoever they may be, have got the music world thinking.”

"Wow," Bobby breathed as the video finished.

"Wow, indeed." Dad ruffled Bobby's curls. "I'm proud of you and your friends."

"Thanks." Bobby smiled.

"Now hurry up or you'll be late for singing class."

Bobby gobbled up his breakfast and then looked up at Dad. "Can you send me the link to that news video?"

"Sure."

"I can't wait to show the others."

As Bobby walked out the door and down the street, his feet pounding a beat on the pavement, he started to hum. A new melody was taking shape in his mind.

Maybe, he thought, it would be fun to turn it into a song with his friends.